Adriel, Marc, and Yuna, sweet dreams.
– *Susanna Isern*

For Pepo, who was always by my side while illustrating this book.
And for Felix, who also accompanied me, inside my belly.
– *Mariana Ruiz Johnson*

Copyright © 2016 Tres Tigres Tristes, an imprint of Publicaciones ilustradas TTT, S.L.
Text copyright © Susanna Isern
Illustrations copyright © Mariana Ruiz Johnson
Translation rights arranged through the VeroK Agency, Barcelona, Spain
Translation copyright © 2018 by Kane Press, Inc.

Publisher's Cataloging-in-Publication data

Names: Isern, Susanna, author. | Johnson, Mariana Ruiz, illustrator.
Title: Queen Panda can't sleep / by Susanna Isern; illustrated by Mariana Ruiz Johnson.
Description: New York, NY: StarBerry Books, an imprint of Kane Press, Inc., 2018.
Identifiers: ISBN 9781635920956 (Hardcover) | 9781635920963 (ebook) | LCCN 2018939000
Summary: When Queen Panda can't sleep, animals from all over the world come to help her.
Subjects: LCSH Bedtime--Fiction. | Pandas--Fiction. | China--Fiction. | Animals--Fiction. | BISAC JUVENILE FICTION /
Bedtime & Dreams | JUVENILE FICTION / Animals / Bears | JUVENILE FICTION / People & Places / Asia
Classification: LCC PZ7.I7744 Que 2018 | DDC [E]--dc23

10 9 8 7 6 5 4 3 2 1

First published in the United States of America in 2018
by StarBerry Books, an imprint of Kane Press, Inc.
Printed in China

StarBerry Books is a trademark of Kane Press, Inc.

Book Design: Michelle Martinez

Visit us online at www.kanepress.com

Like us on Facebook
facebook.com/kanepress

Follow us on Twitter
@KanePress

QUEEN PANDA CAN'T SLEEP

by

SUSANNA ISERN

illustrated by

MARIANA RUIZ JOHNSON

🍓 StarBerry Books

New York

No one in the palace had slept in days. Queen Panda was wide awake, which meant her servants were, too. The exhausted tailors were sewing under the light of the moon. The cook was preparing rice cakes around the clock. The butler was cleaning dust from sunset to dawn. And the royal advisor was writing, continuously, in The Big Book of Advice.

The Queen had been unable to sleep for several nights. Her eyes were so red they looked like cherries. And her head pounded like a drum.

Even worse was her bad mood. From the moment the moon appeared to the time the sun came up, she grumbled.

The Queen's servants couldn't take it any longer. One morning, the royal advisor wrote a decree:

"Anyone who succeeds in making the Queen fall asleep will win a bag of Chinese pearls."

The news flew like a swallow to the farthest corners of the country. It crossed mountains, sailed over seas, and echoed among the clouds. Soon, visitors from around the world began to arrive.

The first to come was a shepherd from the plains of Mongolia. He put up a fence and asked his flock of sheep to jump. The Queen started to count. 1, 2, 3, 4 . . . 100 . . . 500 . . . 1000. . . . Despite all her counting, she didn't even blink.

The next visitor was an ancient Bengali.
She was famous for knowing India's secret
legends, including the ones about sleep.
The storyteller told the Queen the world's
most boring story, but the Queen stayed
wide awake.

Two Kenyans approached next, holding out a comfortable hammock. The Queen lay down on it and the visitors rocked her gently. But instead of falling asleep, she began to feel dizzy and rolled right out of the hammock!

Then appeared an Australian jumper. She drew two tools from her pouch: an enchanted branch from the magical Sleeping Tree and a mask that could make a sunny day look like a moonless night. But after trying out her instruments, all she succeeded in doing was making the Queen's headache worse.

Day after day, night after night, dozens of visitors appeared at the palace. There was a wizard who made sleeping potions. A witch who could hypnotize. And bees who offered their wax for earplugs. Yet no one was able to achieve the royal advisor's goal: getting the Queen to sleep.

The inhabitants of the palace were becoming more and more desperate. If the Queen didn't fall asleep soon, they would all go wild!

Finally, one morning, an Egyptian from the shores of the Nile arrived in court. She stood in front of the Queen, opened her enormous mouth, and let out the biggest yawn ever seen on the face of the earth.

Inevitably, the yawn spread. The royal advisor yawned. Then the cook, the tailor, the butler, the Mongolian shepherd, the ancient Bengali, the Parisian diva, the Kenyans, and the Australian. Then everyone fell fast asleep. . . .

Everyone, that is, except the Queen. She wandered among their sleeping bodies, but as hard as she tried to wake them, no one stirred.

Suddenly, her belly started to grumble. Loudly.

GroooAAAAARRRR!

The Queen was hungry, but the cook was snoring like a dog.

So the Queen headed to the kitchen,
where, for the first time in her life,
she prepared herself a meal.

Throughout the day, she found she had to take care
of everyone's chores in the palace. The harvesting,
the chopping, the sewing, the washing.

And this is how something amazing happened. . . .

While the Queen went about doing her chores, her eyelids began to droop. She felt more and more tired.

And finally, after a full day of very hard work,
Queen Panda got some well-deserved sleep.

Z Z Z Z Z Z